"Kellogg at his best," wrote *Booklist* in a starred review of *Pinkerton, Behave!*, the madcap predecessor to *A Rose for Pinkerton*.

In this hilarious sequel Pinkerton seems lonely. He needs a friend, and a sweet, cuddly kitten like Rose should fill the bill perfectly. But Rose has ideas of her own. *She* wants to be a Great Dane and she's scaring poor Pinkerton out of his wits. As for Pinkerton—he's crawling into the cat carrier, eating cat food, and curling up on people's laps. So it's off to the International Pet Show to seek some expert advice. What results is one of Steven Kellogg's zaniest, funniest romps ever.

Readers who cheered on Pinkerton in *Pinkerton, Behave!* will applaud the return of the lovable Great Dane in Steven Kellogg's newest delight.

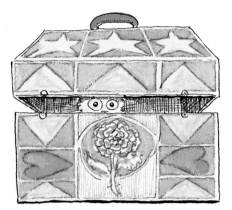

A ROSE FOR PINKERTON

Story and pictures by
STEVEN KELLOGG

The Dial Press   *New York*

Published by The Dial Press
1 Dag Hammarskjold Plaza
New York, New York 10017

Library of Congress Cataloging in Publication Data
Kellogg, Steven / A rose for Pinkerton.
Summary / Pinkerton's family decides he needs a friend,
but is a cat named Rose really suitable?
[1. Dogs—Fiction. 2. Cats—Fiction] I. Title.
PZ7.K292Ro   [E]   81-65848
ISBN 0-8037-7502-4   AACR2
ISBN 0-8037-7503-2 (lib. bdg.)

The process art consists of black line-drawings,
black halftones, and full-color washes. The black line
is prepared and photographed separately for greater
contrast and sharpness. The full-color washes and
the black halftones are prepared with ink, crayons,
and paints on the reverse side of the black line-drawing.
They are then camera-separated and reproduced as
red, blue, yellow, and black halftones.

And another for Helen

Pinkerton, are you lonely? Do you miss curling up with your brothers and sisters?

We should get some other Great Dane puppies to play with Pinkerton.

I think he's trying to tell you that he agrees with me.

One Great Dane is enough! The only other pet I would consider would be something small and quiet...like a goldfish.

I'll go find a friend for you, Pinkerton.

This is the perfect place!

Pinkerton couldn't curl up with a goldfish.

And he couldn't play with a bird.

Maybe a kitten would be just right!

It says here in my book that Great Dane puppies
and kittens can become good friends.

Here's a surprise for you and Pinkerton.
Her name is Rose.

It says in this book by Sarah Chattercat that Great
Dane puppies and kittens can become good friends.

He seems to like her.

Rose took over Pinkerton's sun spot.

She's eating his dinner.

I think Rose wants to be a Great Dane.

Oh, no!

Now Pinkerton is trying to be a kitten!

Let's go back to that pet show! I have a
few questions for Sarah Chattercat!

Rose! Come back!

Pinkerton will be safe with the kittens.
Help me find Rose.

Rose! Where are you?

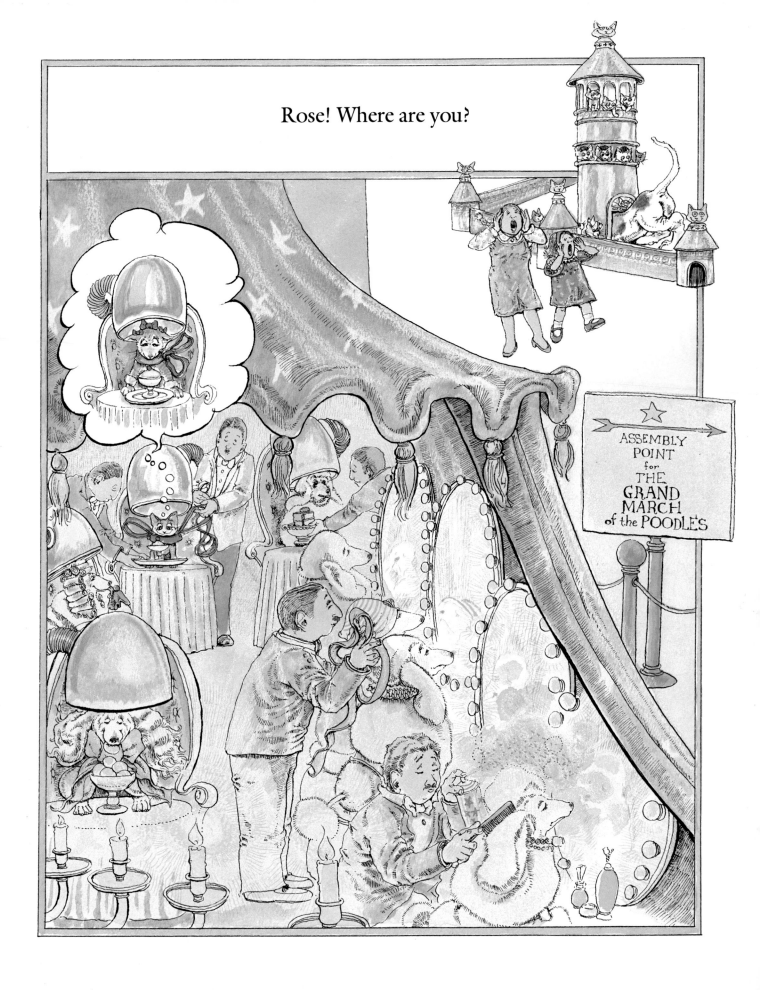

I see her! She's in line for the Grand March of the Poodles!

I'd like to welcome our television audience to this stunning event and to introduce Dr. Aleasha Kibble of Canine University, who will present the Golden Poodle Trophy.

Stop the ceremony! Call the police! The Grand March has been infiltrated by a feline impostor!

Excuse us, but that's our cat, Rose. She used to think she was a Great Dane but she's decided to be a poodle.

Ladies and gentlemen, the crowd and the poodles have gone berserk!

They are chasing the intruding cat toward the Castle of the Kittens!

There's a monster in the Castle of the Kittens.

Arrest that brute! He terrified our poodles,
and they've all fainted!

Nonsense! This wonderful dog saved the kittens.
He's a hero!

Look! It's Rose!

Does she still think she's a poodle?
Or is she a Great Dane again?

She's purring!

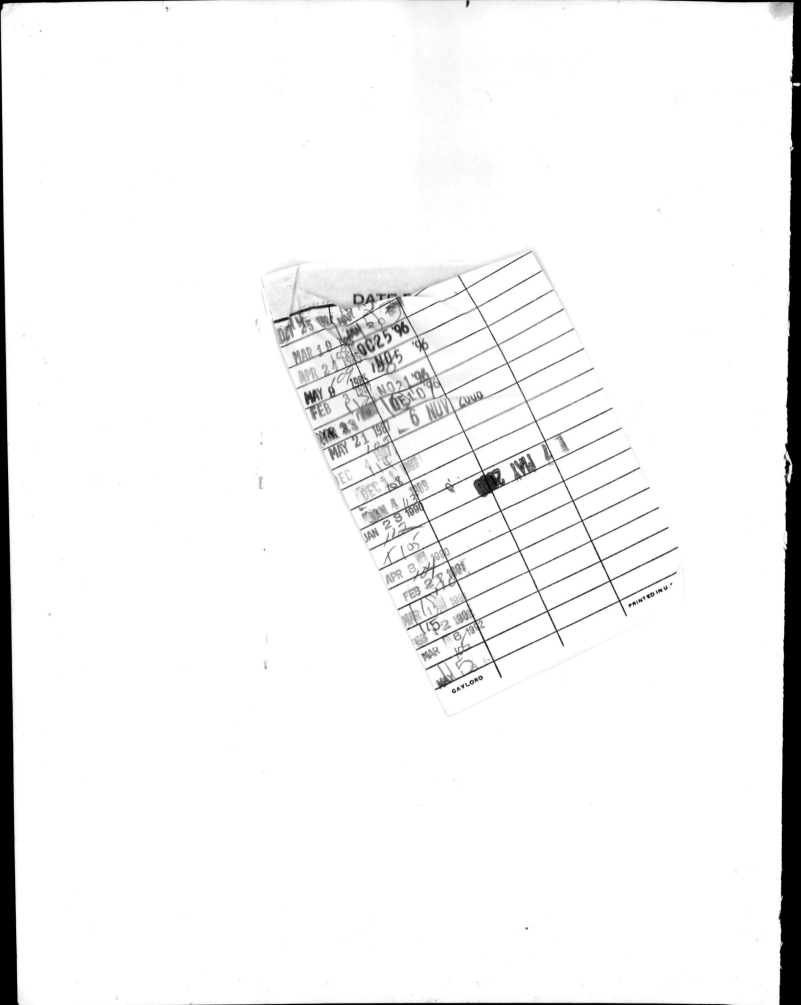